Write Now!

**How to turn
your ideas into
great stories**

D0924674

Write Now!

How to turn your ideas into great stories

Karleen Bradford

Scholastic Canada Ltd.

Scholastic Canada Ltd.
123 Newkirk Road, Richmond Hill, Ontario, Canada L4C 3G5

Scholastic Inc.
555 Broadway, New York, NY 10012, USA

Scholastic Australia Pty Limited
PO Box 579, Gosford, NSW 2250, Australia

Scholastic New Zealand Limited
Private Bag 94407, Greenmount, Auckland, New Zealand

Scholastic Publications Ltd.
Villiers House, Clarendon Avenue, Leamington Spa,
Warwickshire CV32 5PR, UK

Story Starter ideas reprinted from *Meet Canadian Authors and Illustrators* by Allison Gertridge, published by Scholastic Canada Ltd. Copyright © 1994. All rights reserved.

Title page ideas adapted from *The Lettering Book Companion* by Noelene Morris, published by Ashton Scholastic Ltd. Copyright © 1987. All rights reserved.

Design by Andrea Casault

Canadian Cataloguing in Publication Data
Bradford, Karleen
    Write now! : how to turn your ideas into great stories

Previously published under title: Write now! : the
right way to write a story.
ISBN 0-590-24931-2

1. Fiction - Authorship - Juvenile literature.
2. Short story - Juvenile literature. I. Title.

PE1408.B68 1996   j808.3'1   C96-930890-6

6 5 4 3 2 1   Printed in Canada   6 7 8 9/9

Contents

Believe it or not, it's not all that hard

"**W**rite a short story. For next Monday."

Write a short story? For next Monday? You've got to be kidding!

Unfortunately your teacher is not. So how do you do it?

Believe it or not, it's *not* all that hard . . .

✳ ✳ ✳

The first thing you need, of course, is an idea. Search your mind. Right. It's as blank as that blank piece of paper sitting in front of you. So sit back, close your eyes, and *don't* look at the paper. Think. What's been happening in your life lately? I can hear your answer.

"NOTHING!"

That's not true, though. You're alive, aren't you? Then things are happening. You just have to train yourself to see them and to use them.

I like to think of a writer as a big, walking sponge, open to and taking in everything that's going on. Some people walk through their whole lives just looking at what's right in front of them or what's under their noses. Writers look around. They watch people. They wonder about them. They eavesdrop. (Very rude, but writers are allowed. Just don't get caught.) They are aware of what things smell like, what they feel like. Writers are curious, and things *are* happening. All the time. They don't have to be big, monumental, colossal things. Most short stories start from very small beginnings:

Did the dog chew up your mother's brand-new Italian leather purse? Did you have to babysit a rotten kid? Did you have a fight with your best friend? Did your teacher ask you to write a short story?

If you get stuck for ideas, try brainstorming. It works. Pick up your pencil or pen and start jotting things down. You'll have to open your eyes for this, I'm afraid, and tackle that blank piece of paper, but don't bother about making sense. That's not important right now. Just write down any and every idea that crosses your mind.

For example:
- × I've chewed my pencil so hard it looks like a mouse has been at it.
- × I just heard an enormous noise in the kitchen.
- × The doorbell just rang.

And so on and so on and so on. You think they don't sound like ideas for stories? Wait and see what we can do with them.

Clustering (described by Gabrielle Lusser Rico in *Writing the Natural Way*) is a fun way to generate ideas. It feels more like playing than getting down to "the hard work of writing."

This is how you do it:

Think of a word — any word that comes to mind. Write it down in the middle of a big piece of paper. (Even if you usually write on a computer, you'll find it easier to do clustering on a blank piece of paper.) Draw a circle around it. What does that word make you think of? Write that down, draw a circle around it and connect it to the first circle. What does that second word make you think of? Draw a line from the second to the third word or thought and draw a circle around it. Got a brand new idea about what your first word made you think of? Draw a new line from the first word, write down your brand new idea and draw a circle around it. Keep on going.

Here's an example:

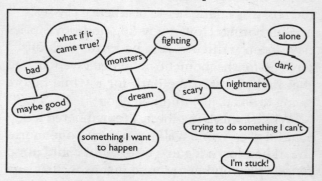

The important thing about clustering is to relax and let yourself play with the ideas or thoughts as they come to you. It doesn't matter one bit if they don't make sense, or even look just crazy. Have a good time with it. We'll see what comes of this later on, too.

Another way to generate ideas is to put your mind to work while you're sleeping. Just because *you're* resting doesn't mean *it* has to.

I was asked to write a short story for a school reader once when I was in the middle of writing a novel and didn't really want to take the time off to write a story. It's very flattering when editors ask you for things, however, so I thought it wouldn't be too bright of me to refuse. Trouble was, I couldn't think of a thing to write about.

What had I been doing lately? Sitting at my typewriter every day writing a book. Interesting for me, perhaps, but for somebody else? Boring!

Then I started thinking. I had also just bought a golden retriever pup, and my thirteen-year-old son was taking her to obedience classes.

Still boring. How many dog-and-boy stories have been written? Must be in the millions. I gave up for the moment, but when I went to bed that night I lay in the dark for a while before going to sleep, just thinking about it.

While I was lying there, I remembered a dog that I'd seen while walking my pup one morning. It had lost a leg in a trap, but it could jump fences, play and get around just as well as any four-legged dog I'd ever seen. Maybe there would be something in that.

I told my mind sternly to work on it during

the night, then went to sleep. Sure enough, when I woke up the next morning, the beginnings of a story were there to greet me.

What if a boy was determined that his beautiful new dog, descended from a long line of champions, was going to be a champion, too? And then what if *his* dog lost a leg in a trap? Magic words, those: "What if . . .?" Every writer knows them well. What would the boy do? What would the dog do?

I sat down at my typewriter, sketched out a very rough outline (more about that later), and a short story emerged out of a space in my head that the day before had been as empty as a picture of a polar bear in a snowstorm.

Your problems, fears and worries are still another source inside you for stories. If you're a human being you must have them. Probably lots of them sometimes.

I nearly drowned once trying to rescue my dog (same dog) after she'd fallen through the ice. I found that for a week or so afterwards I couldn't get to sleep at night, or if I did, I'd wake up in the middle of the night and not be able to get back to sleep again.

It seemed every time I closed my eyes I was back in that lake, alone in a vast, deserted park early in the morning, with the weight of my coat and boots dragging me down again and again.

Finally, one day I sat down and wrote a story about a boy who almost drowned while trying to save his dog. I called it *Not Ever Again*.

It was an exciting story, and it served a good purpose in warning kids pretty graphically about the dangers of going out on the ice. But it did something else far more important for me. It allowed me to get my fears and feelings out onto paper, and from then on I could sleep. (Dog didn't have these problems. Dog had acted like the whole thing was fun, once I was in there with her.)

Think about your own problems and fears, then try writing about them. You can disguise the people and the situations if they're too personal. As an added bonus, in addition to finding that you've come up with a good idea for a short story, you might even find that you've come up with some answers or solutions for yourself.

I think that's called "killing two birds with one stone," although I don't particularly like the image that conjures up. (Might make a good idea for a story, though. What if someone *did* kill two birds with one stone . . .?)

Try This!

1. Be a sponge. Watch, and listen, and smell things. Be curious.

   Get yourself a brand-new notebook. Open it and give it a good sniff. (There's nothing nicer than the smell of a brand-new, sparkling clean notebook.)

   - Sit for a while and stare at it.
   - Think about everything that's happened to you lately, good or bad.
   - Think about everything you wish would happen to you.
   - Jot down as many thoughts as you can.

   (You can do this on your computer, too, if you want. Set up a directory of documents especially for your writing projects.)

2. Turn to a new page. In the middle of it, write the first word that comes into your mind. Draw a circle around it, and CLUSTER.

3. Last thing before you go to sleep, think about everything you've soaked up while you've been being a sponge, look over what you've written in your notebook, put your mind to work on it and go to sleep. Happy dreams!

Take a problem, stir well

Now let's take some of those ideas and play around with them a little.

- × The dog chewing up your mother's purse, for example. What did your mom think about that? What did the cat think about it?
- × What about babysitting the rotten kid? What did she do? What did you do?
- × Fighting with your best friend? What was it all about? How did you feel? How did your best friend feel? What if it was all over a misunderstanding, but neither of you knew that?
- × Your teacher asking you to write a short story? What if the school fell down — would you still have to hand in that story?
- × While chewing your pencil you accidentally swallow the eraser and start to choke to death and there's nobody else home. (I know, I know. That's a bit far-fetched, but we're just fooling around here.)
- × There's an enormous noise in the

kitchen but (again) you are alone in the house and you *know* there shouldn't be anyone in there. Did you remember to lock the back door when you came home?

* The doorbell just rang. It's either that friend you were fighting with, or your mom, who forgot her keys and is about to find her purse all chewed up, or . . . or . . . or . . .

* What about that clustering? What if a boy had a really scary dream, and what if it came true . . .?

So far these have just been aimless ramblings, but by now something will have struck a spark. There's a glimmer of interest there somewhere. Pounce on it. You've got a problem of some kind? Make it worse! A story has to have a plot, and that's what this is all about. What happened? What happened next? And then what happened after that? How does it all turn out? Choose one of your ideas and take it further.

* Your mom didn't want the dog in the first place. She likes cats instead. She's bound to make you get rid of it now. (The cat, by the way, is looking very smug.)

* After you finish cleaning up the mess that rotten kid made, you suddenly realize you haven't been keeping an eye

on her — and now she's disappeared!

× You decide to apologize to your friend, but before you can, you find out she's been telling lies about you — and you get mad all over again.

× Not only has the school fallen down, but you are trapped in the same room with your teacher and he's badly hurt.

× The pencil idea does seem bad enough at the moment, so maybe we don't need to make that problem worse just yet.

× There's definitely someone — or some-*thing* — in the kitchen!

× The boy dreams his house is on fire and he gets out, but then runs back in for his dog and is trapped inside.

You've got your problem all set, and getting worse by the minute. Now it's time to stop writing and start thinking again. What are you going to do with this? Does it turn out funny, bad or sad? What do you want to happen, and how are you going to make it happen?

Don't worry if you don't know all the answers right now. You'd be surprised at how many writers don't know how their stories are going to turn out. There have been lots of times when I've said to myself after writing all morning, "How interesting. I didn't know that was going to happen!"

You might want to walk around and think about your story for a while at this point, or just sit and stare out the window. (My family still doesn't quite believe me when they walk into my room and find me sitting comfortably in a chair with my eyes closed and I tell them I'm *working*.)

You might even want to sleep on it again. When you do start getting it clear in your mind, it's time to face that paper once more and start jotting your thoughts down, even if it's only in point form.

Be sure you write them down, though. Don't count on remembering them later. I know from bitter experience that you probably won't. After having forgotten several ideas that I'm sure were absolutely, totally wonderful, I now keep a pencil and notebook with me all the time — even beside my bed at night.

Just the act of writing down all the ideas you've had so far will help you think of new ones, then you can start to get your story in order.

Try This!

1. Look over the ideas and thoughts you've jotted down, and choose one of them.

2. Stare out the window, or close your eyes, and think about it for a while. What's the main problem going to be?

3. Write down the idea you've chosen on a fresh page in your notebook (or in your computer document), and add your problem.

4. Keep your pencil or pen and notebook handy during the day and beside your bed at night. Be ready for more ideas to strike at any hour.

5. Write down the idea you've chosen on a fresh page in your notebook (or in your computer document), and add your problem.

6. Keep your pencil or pen and notebook handy during the day and beside your bed at night. Be ready for more ideas to strike at any hour.

Think of
a skeleton,
not a cage

Outlines: sometimes you need them, sometimes you don't. Sometimes an idea for a story will come to you so complete and finished that all you have to do is sit there and try to write fast enough to keep up with it. That has happened to me, but only once or twice. Usually I have to organize my story before I start writing it. That's when I need to make an outline.

Start by jotting down the original idea that you've now settled on, the problem that you've invented and the complications you've already dreamed up. Then write down what you think will happen and how it will end (if you know).

Now expand on it as much as possible. How do the characters in your story feel about what's happening? Put that down. What do they do about it? Put that down. What happens in the end (if you know by now)? Get it all down.

As an example, let me go back to my three-legged dog story and show you how my outline for that developed. First I started with just the bare details:

✗ Boy owns a valuable pedigreed golden retriever. (Original idea.)

- ✗ Dog loses leg. (Problem.)
- ✗ Boy wanted dog to be a show dog. (Complication.)
- ✗ Ending???????????

Next I expanded on that in a second outline.

- ✗ Boy owns a valuable pedigreed golden retriever.
- ✗ Dog loses leg. (How? Possibly caught in a trap in the woods. Boy doesn't find dog for days. How many days? Find out from vet how long a dog must be in a trap to lose its leg but still be able to live.)
- ✗ Dog lives. Boy still loves dog, but is terribly disappointed that it will never be a champion now.
- ✗ Dog learns to get along on three legs better than most dogs could on five. Loves obedience training and is extremely good at it.
- ✗ Boy decides to enter dog in obedience trials and make it a champion that way.

Here I ran into a problem. Talking to the trainer at my own dog's obedience school, I found out that you can't enter a dog even in obedience trials unless it is "sound of limb." At that point my story seemed to have come to a dead end.

Then the trainer told me there were informal club obedience trials, the only difference being that the dog wouldn't become a recognized champion if he won them.

My immediate response was, "Oh, this boy wouldn't want that for his dog. He wants the 'real thing.'"

Then my mind started working again, and here's how the outline went on:

* Boy finds out dog can't enter regular obedience trials.
* Trainer suggests boy enter dog in club trials because the dog is so well trained and loves the work so much.
* Boy rejects this angrily. That's not good enough for *his* dog.
* Trainer keeps insisting and finally, seeing how much fun the dog has doing obedience work, boy gives in and enters dog in club trials.
* Dog wins. (Is that it? Seems blah. Needs something more. Maybe it'll come to me as I write.)

Outlines help you get going with your story, and also show you where you might have to do some research before you actually start writing, as you can see from this example.

If, later on, your story suddenly takes off and things start happening that you didn't know were going to happen — if the characters take over and start doing what *they* want to do instead of what you intended them to do — great!

It'll mean your story is coming alive — and that's just what you want it to do.

In that case, change your outline or expand it. It's not engraved in stone. An outline is meant to help you, not make things harder. Think of it as a skeleton that you can build on, not as a cage that hems you in and keeps you trapped.

Keep in mind while you're jotting down your outline that your story is going to have to have interesting characters, conflict (your main character's problem), a plot that will keep your readers interested, and — sooner or later — you're going to have to figure out an ending. We'll talk about all of these in the chapters to come.

❋ ❋ ❋

With this dog story, by the time I'd finished the outline and started writing, I knew it would end with the dog winning. But I didn't know at that point *how* the dog would win. I just knew it was going to have to be something special.

When I got the boy to the club trials, which he still viewed with contempt, I was as surprised as he to find out that he was, in fact, as nervous as if the trials were "all for real."

The dog then took over my writing and just romped through those trials, having such a wonderful time that it won the whole thing. At the end, the judge announced that he had never awarded so many points to *any* other dog in *any* other show, formal or informal, before.

Then — I could see it as clearly as could be — the dog sat there in the winners' circle, balanced precariously on three legs, tongue lolling out of the widest laughing mouth possible on any breed of dog, and all the people around stood up and cheered.

The something special that I had needed had come to me while I wrote. The outline had worked. It had pointed the way. After that, the story had just taken over and gone there.

Try This!

1. New page. Jot down your original idea, the problem you've invented, any other complications you can think of, and the ending (if you know it; don't worry if you don't).

2. Another new page. (Now you see why you needed a brand-new, empty notebook, or a special document in your computer. We're using a lot of space here.) At the top of your page write OUTLINE.

   Now expand on your story idea as much as you possibly can, in point form. Cross out, erase, make as much of a mess as you want. It's your notebook, and there are still lots of pages left. Make as many outlines as you want. Use a separate page for each. (Date them, too, so you always know which is your most recent version.)

Who's who and which is what?

You've got your outline. You've got at least a vague idea of what your story is going to be all about. But who is in it? Who is the main character? What is his or her name? What is he or she like? Who are the other characters? What are their names? What are they like? How old are all these people? How long have they known each other?

A quick tip here. Don't load a short story down with too many characters — there isn't room. In a long novel you can bring in lots of people, but in a short story it's probably better to stick with one main character and one or two secondary characters. Make sure that any other people who walk into your story are really necessary. If they're not — walk them right back out. You haven't got time or space for them.

Start with the main character. You might want to make it your own self, or you might want to make it someone else. If you decide on someone else, then the first and most important thing is to find out the character's name.

Sometimes a name will just come to you. Sometimes you'll have to search for it. Once you've got it, write it down. Then underneath, write down everything you possibly can about this person.

It doesn't matter if you end up using only some of this information in your story. The important thing is to get to know this person as well as you know your own best friend — or better. When you do, you'll know how your hero or heroine will feel about the problems you've created, and possibly even how he or she will go about solving them.

Now do the same thing with every other person in your story (including the animals).

Quite often you'll find that while you're writing the story, somebody you didn't think was going to be important will gradually become more and more so.

This happened in one of my books. A girl who was going to be a minor character developed a very strong personality and finally became just as important as the two main characters. In fact, I had to keep her under control or she would have run away with the whole story! (Actually, I became so fond of her that I might just give her a book of her own one of these days.)

If you really get to know your characters as well as you possibly can, you'll find that they'll sometimes do their own talking. All you'll have to do is write the words down. If you try to make them say or do something that isn't right for them, they'll refuse!

I've often had times when things just

wouldn't work out. And each time, after sitting back and taking a good look at what I was doing, I've realized that I was trying to make a person do or say something that was completely out of character.

I'd suddenly think, Jane (or Jim, or whoever) would never say that! She'd never do that! That's what the problem is!

I'd go back to my notes on Jane, start thinking once more about what kind of person she was, and try to figure out what the appropriate reaction would *really* be. Then I'd start writing again, and finally it would come out right.

Of course, if you decide to make yourself a character — perhaps even the main character — there's no need to write a sketch about yourself, is there? You know yourself, right?

Wrong! Just because you've decided to base a character on yourself doesn't mean that you have to tell the whole, complete, literal truth about yourself.

For the sake of your story you might want to change lots of things around. You could make yourself better than you really are, or worse. You could make yourself do all the wonderful things you wish you could, or say all the clever things you wish you had — or you could let yourself go and do something really nasty or bad that you would never dream of doing (or have the nerve to do) in real life.

You don't have to tell the truth. You can decide who's who and what's going to happen.

You're writing the story and you're in control.

When my daughter was very young and I punished her once for lying, she said resentfully, "When I grow up, I'm going to be a writer and then I can lie all I want."

That's part of the fun of being a writer. In fact, you're *expected* to tell "lies." The truth is rarely interesting enough. You can change it around as much as you want in a story. You can change people, even yourself, to your heart's content.

But be careful if you decide to use yourself in a story. Something just might happen that I think I'd better warn you about. In the same way that you sometimes find out more about your characters while you're writing about them (even when you thought you knew them perfectly well before you started), you might also find out something more about *yourself* than you knew when you started. Rather scary idea, that, sometimes. On the other hand, it can also be pretty interesting. Life is all about growing up and getting to know yourself, and writing is all about life. It might very well be that after you finish writing a story you could read it and think: I didn't realize I felt so strongly about that! Or, even: I didn't realize that's what I felt at all!

Another variation on this theme is to write in the first person (using "I," that is), but making it someone *other* than yourself.

You may actually be a girl named Mary, but decide to write a story from the point of view of a boy named Tom. Why not? It would be interesting to see if you could do it. If you are a boy, could you write from a girl's point of view? You might learn a lot from such an experience.

If you do a good job of getting to know your characters, the people who read your stories will feel that *they* have gotten to know your characters too. They'll believe in them and care about what happens to them.

When I finish a story, and even more so when I finish a long book, I often feel sad. I've come to know the young people in my stories so well that I don't want to say goodbye to them. I feel I'm going to miss them almost as much as I would miss my own children. In fact, in very many ways, the children in my books *are* my own children.

The characters you create will be your own children too, and your best friends. Even, sometimes, your enemies. The most important thing is, they will be real.

Try This!

1. Start a new page. (How did you know I was going to say that?) Write the name of your main character at the top; then, in point form or in essay form, whichever you prefer, write as much as you can about that character. Include:

   - Age
   - Physical description
   - Emotional characteristics (shy, aggressive, self-confident, bullying?)
   - Favourite things
   - Most hated things
   - Best friend
   - Worst enemy
   - Does he or she like school? Is he or she good at school?
   - How does he or she feel about his or her parents?
   - Favourite sport
   - Favourite hobbies

   Add as many things as you can to this list.

2. Draw a picture of your character, if you want. Or try painting or sculpting your

character — just "spending time" with a character in this way can help you find out more about his or her personality.

3. Write down a favourite expression that only this character uses. It could be "Awesome!" or "No way!" or "You know?" or anything else you can think of.

4. Describe a particular habit that only this character has. Maybe a boy tosses his hair out of his eyes all the time. Or a girl twirls her hair around her finger, or chews on the ends. (This could drive another of your characters crazy.) Your character could raise one eyebrow when he or she doesn't believe something. (I've always wanted to be able to do this!) Perhaps she bites her nails when she's nervous, and is trying to break the habit. Perhaps he drums on tables, chairs, whatever is handy. (This could also drive another character crazy.)

5. Do this for each character in your story.

Let's talk!

Dialogue. It's important that it sound natural. This doesn't mean writing the way people actually talk, though. Take a few moments to listen to the conversations around you. Chances are you won't hear one complete sentence. And it's more than likely that people are interrupting each other, and finishing each other's sentences, all the time. If you wrote their dialogue down word for word it would be a terrible mishmash. So the trick is to organize what your characters say to each other in such a way that it *sounds* natural, but also makes sense.

You can have one person interrupt another when necessary, however. Use a dash at the end of the sentence.

For example:

"You never listen to a word I —" Michelle began.

"Of course I do," Jim interrupted.

Or if a person is lost in thought and their words trail off, use three dots:

"I wonder if I could find out what's really going on . . ." Mary's voice trailed away.

There are lots of ways to avoid repeating "said." Some of them could be:

"I — I don't believe that," Jane stuttered.

"I *can't* believe that!" Susan exclaimed.

"No, I won't," Ted answered.

"Okay," Joe replied.

"NO!" Mary screamed.

"Get out!" Chris shouted.

"I'm afraid," Barbara whispered.

Be careful about going too far with this, however. A lot of the time "said" is the easiest and quickest word to use, and chances are if the action is zipping along your reader will not even notice it.

Avoid using verbs that are impossible, such as:

"I hope not," Mary sighed.

"That's ridiculous," Tim laughed.

Just try sighing a sentence, or laughing a sentence. It can't be done. Instead you could put it this way:

"I hope not." Mary sighed.

"That's ridiculous." Tim let out a bellow of laughter.

Avoid adverbs as much as you possibly can, such as "laughed happily" or "sobbed sadly." You can be fairly certain that if someone's laughing, it's happily, or if sobbing, it's sadly. If your verb doesn't seem clear or specific enough without the adverb, try a different verb that's more precise.

It's not always necessary to use a dialogue tag such as "said" or "shouted." You can let the character's actions tell the reader who is speaking.

For example:
"I hate this school and everybody in it!" Beth slammed her books down on her desk so hard a couple of them bounced off and landed on the floor.

"I'm sorry, I can't tell you that." Jim turned his back on Ted and walked away.

Use your dialogue to further the action and tell your readers something more about the person who is speaking, or what is going on. The dialogue above lets us know exactly how Beth is feeling, without the need for the author to tell the reader that Beth is angry. The reader can see that very well. The dialogue also lets us know that Jim has a secret he can't share with Ted. Again, we haven't told the reader that, we have *shown* it through what Jim says. "Show, don't tell," is a good rule to remember when writing.

Sometimes, if there are only two people talking and you want the action to move quickly, you don't need to identify who is speaking after every sentence, just once in a while to keep the reader on track.

For example:

"I didn't steal it!" Don's face was flushed with anger.

"Yeah, right. Then how come it's in your locker?" Dave shot back. He looked just as mad.

"I don't know. I don't know how it got there." Don was almost shouting now.

"You expect me to believe that?"

"Yes. It's the truth!"

"Well, I don't believe you. Sorry."

"You have to!" To his horror, Don realized there were tears in his eyes.

We mentioned in the last chapter that each of your characters could have one distinctive thing that only he or she says. Develop this further, and make sure that each of your characters speaks in his or her own way. Your reader should be able to tell that it is Mary speaking rather than Susan by what she's saying, or *how* she's saying it. Perhaps Mary is a little hesitant and speaks shyly, while Susan just blasts away without regard for anyone else's feelings. Perhaps Jim can't help bragging, while Tom apologizes for everything. Perhaps Mike contradicts everything anybody else says. Maybe Beth is a peacemaker, always trying to smooth things over. The way they talk will reflect this.

It is very important to remember when writing your story that each time a new character speaks you must start a new paragraph. If you don't, your reader will get confused. Starting a new paragraph each time another character speaks lets the reader know that a different person is now talking. Just look at the difference in the next two examples:

"I can't find my homework project," Linda cried. "Where did you leave it last night?" her mother answered. "Right here in my room. I know I did!" Linda dug through the mess on her desk.

"I can't find my homework project," Linda cried.

"Where did you leave it last night?" her mother answered.

"Right here in my room. I know I did!" Linda dug through the mess on her desk.

Which is easier to read? Did you get a little lost in the first one? This rule applies even when the sentence is only one word:

"Want to come with me?" Jerry asked.

"No," Fred answered.

"Why not?"

"Can't."

Imagine if you squished that all up. It would come out like this: "Want to come with me?" Jerry asked. "No," Fred answered. "Why not?" "Can't."

Doesn't make too much sense, does it?

Try This!

1. Write a page or two of dialogue between the main characters in your story. Try to find good strong verbs that let you avoid using "said" too often, and also tell your reader how your character feels, or what is going on.

2. See if you can recognize who is speaking by the way he or she talks, even if you don't identify them. (You could try writing half a page of dialogue without dialogue tags, to see if your characters' ways of speaking identify them clearly.)

Whose story is this, and when is it happening?

We mentioned point of view in Chapter 4. Let's explore that a bit more. You may be a girl named Mary writing from the point of view of a boy named Tom, or a boy writing from a girl's point of view. It doesn't matter. You're a writer. You're allowed.

But first of all, let's decide whether you're going to tell your story in the first person or in the third. Let's say you're going to tell the story from Tom's point of view. If you write it in the first person, you will be using "I."

For example:
My name is Thomas, but everybody calls me Tom. Except my mom. She insists on Thomas. I hate that.

If you write it in the third person, you will be using Tom's name.

For example:
Tom's real name is Thomas, but everybody calls him Tom. Except his mom. She insists on Thomas. He hates that.

It's up to you to choose which one you feel more comfortable with, and which is more suitable for your story.

I can hear you asking: "What is the second person?" Well, it's "you," and it's pretty hard to write a story from that point of view, although it can be done.

For example:
Your real name is Thomas, but everybody calls you Tom. Except your mom. She insists on Thomas. You hate that.

Sounds weird, doesn't it?

Once you've decided whose point of view you're going to write from, the most important — and hardest — thing to do is to stick to it. This means that you have to be inside that character's head for every minute of your story. You can only see what that character sees, hear what that character hears. If a fight is going on three blocks away, your character won't know what's happening unless somebody tells him or her. Your character doesn't know what other people are thinking — he or she can only imagine it.

If you skip around from one character's point of view to another, your reader is going to get thoroughly confused. Look at the following beginning for a story, and you'll see what I mean:

From the minute Mary woke up, she knew it was going to be a bad day. She tripped over a pile of books she'd left lying on the floor beside her bed, and her mother had cooked lumpy oatmeal for breakfast. Things just got worse. When she walked into her classroom, Jim was sitting at her desk. He knew she hated that!

Okay, obviously this is Mary's story and we're comfortably inside her head and ready to find out what's going to happen to her next. However . . .

Jim looked up. Mary seemed mad. I don't care, he thought. I've had a rotten night — another fight with my father — and I'll just sit wherever I want.

Oops! Maybe this is Jim's story. We seem to be inside *his* head now. Okay. But . . .

Tom walked in. Jim and Mary were fighting again. As usual. Those two could never get on, he thought. He wished they'd give it a break.

Wait a minute! Now we're inside Tom's head, looking at things from *his* point of view. Whose story *is* this anyway?

Very confusing for your reader.

There is a way to stay inside your main character's viewpoint and still give your reader a good idea of what's going on with the other characters.

For example:

Mary walked into the classroom. Jim was sitting at her desk. He knew she hated that. He was scowling. Probably had another fight with his dad, Mary thought. His dad really gave him a hard time. She didn't care, though, he had no business messing up her desk. She stormed over.

"Hey, you guys." A voice from the doorway startled her just as she was beginning to let Jim know exactly how she felt. "Give it a break, will you? You two never stop fighting!"

It was Tom. Butting in as usual.

Your reader gets a good idea of what both Jim and Tom are thinking, but it's from Mary's point of view.

Of course this would work just as well in the first person, if that's how you feel more comfortable. Just start off:

From the moment I woke up, I knew it was going to be a bad day. I tripped over a pile of books I'd left lying by my bed, and Mom had made lumpy oatmeal for breakfast.

Carry on from there. You might find out that for some stories you feel more comfortable writing in first person, while for others, third person seems better. Trust your instinct for which one works best for your story.

Sometimes you can write from more than one point of view, but you have to know that you're doing it, and not do it by accident. Books that do this will have a different structure. They might have a chapter headed DAVID, and that chapter will be from David's point of view. The next might be ANDREW, and that chapter will be from Andrew's point of view. This lets the reader know that the point of view is changing. There usually has to be a very good reason for doing this, though. Perhaps it's absolutely necessary, for the story to work, to get inside both those boys' heads completely. Otherwise, stick to the single point of view.

There is one other point of view that is not used very much now, but used to be. It's the omniscient (all knowing) point of view. That is where the author knows everything that's going on, including what everybody is thinking, and tells the reader. These books often used to start out something like this:

Now, dear reader, let me tell you what happened in the year 1816 to a family named Jacobs . . .

Fairytales were usually from this point of view. Remember:

Once upon a time there lived a beautiful girl who had a mean stepmother and two ugly stepsisters . . .

You can use the omniscient point of view if you want to. Again, just be sure you know what you're doing, you structure it carefully, and you're not just doing things by accident and mixing them up.

❋ ❋ ❋

Now let's talk about tenses. Most stories are written in the past tense, like this:

> Dave tried to tell himself to calm down. It's just a game, he thought. It doesn't matter if we win or lose. But somehow he couldn't make himself believe that.

Even if you start out in the present tense by describing yourself or someone else, who is presumably still alive, you switch into the past when you actually start the story. For example:

> I'm not the shy type, and I'm not nervous about meeting new people at all, but last week was different. I had to go to a party where there was no one else there that I knew. I woke up that morning and my stomach felt sick . . .

Or:

> Jim's so tall he has to stoop down to go through doors. He hates that. Last week at our school dance he wouldn't even dance, he was so self-conscious. Instead, he just hung around the food table all night . . .

You can write in the present all the way through if you want. It's difficult, but it might be interesting to try! It would go something like this:

I'm walking to school and I'm not happy. Mary comes up to meet me and she sees that I'm upset. I am not going to tell her why, though. We go into our classroom. The class starts . . .

Use whichever tense you want — although I strongly suggest you stay away from the future tense. That would get you into a lot of complicated trouble.

Let's just try it:
Jeff will wake up and go to school today. He will eat breakfast and then he will find out that his bicycle has a flat tire.

"Darn!" he will say. "I'm going to be late for school!"

He will be late for school and his teacher will say . . .

I've never written in this tense, and I don't think I ever will.

Try This!

1. Take your main character and your outline. Write two paragraphs, one in the first person and one in the third. See which you feel more comfortable with.

For example:

a) Mary was chewing on her hair so hard she didn't hear the homework assignment, so after school she called Stacy to see if she had been listening. Stacy hadn't either.

"What are we going to do?" Mary wailed.

b) I was chewing on my hair so hard I didn't hear the homework assignment, so after school I called Stacy to see if she had been listening. She hadn't either.

"What are we going to do?" I wailed.

2. Play around with the tense if you like, too:

I'm chewing on my hair so hard I don't hear the homework assignment, so after school I call Stacy to see if she knows what it is. She doesn't.

"What are we going to do?" I wail.

Write until you find which voice and tense suits you best. Play around. Experiment!

It's hard to
dive into
cold water

Now, finally, we've done enough sneaking up on this story and we're going to start it. You can write your story in your notebook. If you do, double space it, so that there is room to revise and correct as you go along. You might prefer to write on single sheets of paper; double space here as well. Or you might use a computer. Choose whatever you feel comfortable with. If you write on the computer, don't mess around with the typefaces at this stage. Choose a basic typeface and stick with it; otherwise, you might find yourself spending all your time and energy making your story *look* good, instead of making the story *itself* good.

I use a computer now, although I wrote my first four books on a manual typewriter. When I got an electric typewriter I thought that was the height of luxury; now I couldn't do without my computer. I still print out as I go along, though (I'm doing it right now), and make a lot of my revisions on the printed paper.

Whatever method you use, let's get that story started. Again, nothing that you write is engraved in stone, so don't be afraid to plunge in and put words down. You can always change them later — in fact, you probably will — so just *get going*.

Think about the best books and stories you've ever read. Think about what made you choose those books or stories to read in the first place. Chances are it was the very first page or two. By the same token, you'll want your readers to be so interested by *your* first page that they'll just have to read on.

You'll also want to let your readers know as soon as you can *who* the story is about, *where* the story takes place, and *what* the problem or conflict is.

Introduce your main character, tell enough about him or her to let your readers know at least approximately how old he or she is, let your readers know where the setting is, and then bring on the problem.

Of course, you're not just going to say, "John Wigglestooth is nine years old and lives at 22 Maple Lane and his dog has just chewed up his mother's purse." There's no drama in that, but there are lots of ways to get all the information in *while* you're getting your story going.

One way is to begin with *action!* Mom finding her chewed-up purse. The rotten kid pushing the cat into the toilet. The walls falling down around you and your teacher. A loud crash in the kitchen, or even just the doorbell ringing.

How about:
I had to write a story by Monday, and here

it was, Sunday night already. I was so nervous that I'd chewed my pencil until it looked as if a mouse had been at it. The eraser tasted disgusting, but I hardly even noticed it.

Suddenly, without warning, it came off in my mouth. At that very same moment, I hiccupped — and it lodged in my windpipe. I couldn't breathe!

Gasping for breath, I doubled over my desk. Air! I needed air before I choked to death. But I couldn't do anything. I needed help! Then the awful realization came over me that I was all alone in the house. There was nobody around to help!

Your readers know *who* the story is about (another kid, probably about the same age), *where* the story is taking place (in the main character's room at a desk), and you have certainly introduced the problem.

Another way is to begin with dialogue. Don't *tell* about the fight you and your best friend had; let whoever is reading your story *hear* it. Write it all down in quotes, as furious and bad-tempered and noisy as you can make it.

For example:
"You *lied* about me, Sue Parker. To the whole school! You *lied!*"

"I did not! That's the lie and *you're* telling it!"

Sue had been my best friend for the past eight years — ever since kindergarten — and we'd never fought before. But she'd never lied about me before, either.

You've given your readers all the important facts in the first few lines, and mainly through dialogue. You haven't even had to stop to identify the speakers, either, because the way you've written it makes it obvious who's who.

If you're going to write about the dog episode, try starting with a loud scream . . .

"EEEEEEEEEEEEEK!!!!!!!!!!!!!!!"
The scream came from David's mother in the living room. At exactly the same time his brand-new pup flew into his room and scrambled under the bed, heading for the farthest corner. David had a horrible sinking feeling in the pit of his stomach.
"One more thing," his mother had said. "If that pup chews one more thing, he goes right back to the pound!"
The cat walked by, tail waving complacently. She looked smug.

How about the boy who dreamed he was trapped in the burning house? It could start like this:

For a moment Jeff lay confused. He couldn't figure out what had awakened him. He coughed. He coughed again. There was a tight, suffocating feeling in his chest. As he pulled himself groggily from the last remnants of sleep, he became aware of an acrid, burning smell. His eyes were watering, the insides of his nostrils stinging. Then, suddenly, he was wide awake. His room was full of smoke! The house was on fire!

Once in a while a flashback can be a good way to start off. I had a problem with one of my books. The story was about a young girl, Lady Jane Grey, who was Queen of England for nine days when she was only fifteen. But then the rightful queen, Mary, took her prisoner and ordered her head chopped off. (This is a true story, by the way. It happened in the year 1554.)

My problem was that the story had to start when Jane is nine years old, but most of the story takes place when she is older. I wanted people to know this. I didn't want to start with her being nine years old, or people would think the whole book was going to be about a nine-year-old girl, not a teenager. I solved the problem by the use of a flashback.

The story opens with sixteen-year-old Jane standing at the window of a house overlooking Tower Green, watching a scaffold being erected. She knows she is to be executed there that morning. Then I have her think back to how it all began.

She remembers the day when she was nine years old and the messenger came from London with the news that her cousin Edward, exactly the same age as she, was now King of England, and that she was to go and live at court. The story picks up from there and then goes on until it gets back to the exact moment when it started.

Once, with another book, I had a terrible time with the first chapter. I wrote it and rewrote it and rewrote it and couldn't get it right. Finally I just gave up and went on with the story.

When I finished the book, I went back to rewrite the first chapter, and this time it worked. I guess I just had to get to know my characters a little better — and know what the book was all about a little better — before I could know how it should begin.

Take your idea and start experimenting with first paragraphs. Write two or three, or even more. Try several different ways until you find the way that seems to suit your story best.

The only way a story ever gets written is by starting it, so take a deep breath and dive in!

Try This!

1. Write the first page of your story. Try to let your reader know who the story is about, where the story is taking place and, if possible, what the problem is.

2. If it doesn't seem to work, try again and again until it does. Experiment with voice and tense. You might have to write several pages of "warm-ups" until you get it just right. That's okay. You have to do warm-ups before you start a race, don't you? Sometimes you have to do them before you can really get into your story, too. Just remember to toss them out when you've found the right way to begin, and then start where the story starts.

3. If it's really not working, just go on to the next chapter. Sometimes you have to write the whole story before you can get the beginning right. Don't give up too soon, though. Just trying will help you figure things out in your own mind.

Stuck . . .

You're off to a great start, everything is going along along fine, but suddenly the words stop coming. You know where you want to go — but how are you going to get there? What do you write next? You've ground to a halt. You're out of ideas. You're STUCK.

There's a name for this. It's called "writer's block," and it hits all of us sooner or later. I know, because I've wrestled with it many times. I sit down at the computer and just can *not* think of what I want to say next.

There are lots of ways to deal with this, however, so don't despair. Just consider yourself in the company of most of the writers in the world and learn a few tips from them.

The first thing to do is to *sit down at that desk!* If you walk around saying, "Oh, I just don't feel like writing today. I'll wait until I can think of something," that will be the end of your story. I've read dozens of articles by well-known and even very famous writers who say that the hardest part of writing is actually sitting down and getting to it. It's even harder when you know you're stuck.

I've been known to wash the kitchen floor in

order to avoid my computer on some occasions, and if you were a member of my family you'd know how much I hate that particular chore. In fact, my son came home from school once, walked into the kitchen, and said, "Uh-oh, Mom must be stuck with her writing again. The kitchen floor's clean!"

Sitting down at that desk when it's the last thing in the world you want to do — when you're *afraid* to sit down at it — is called discipline. That's a word that's far more important to writers than the word "talent." You can be the most talented writer in the world, but without discipline you'll never get anything finished.

On the other hand, you may not consider that you have any talent for writing at all, but if you discipline yourself to try, you may surprise yourself and turn out something really good.

Once you're sitting at that desk, what do you do? You could start brainstorming again. What if this happened . . .? What if that happened . . .?

David and his mother have just had a terrible fight. She's ordered him to take the dog back to the pound. You know you want him to keep that dog, but how are you going to make him do it?

Start scribbling down any idea that comes into your mind that might solve the problem. Just the *act* of writing will generate more ideas.

Another trick is to start moving your character around. Make him do something, even if you don't think it has anything to do with your story. I got stuck quite early on in my book about Lady

Jane Grey. I'd written the first chapter, got Jane and her family to London, and was all set to write about the young King Edward's coronation. Then I stalled.

How was I going to get them to the coronation? What should they do next? I sat and stared at the blank piece of paper with "CHAPTER 2" written on it, and bit my fingernails. That wasn't very productive, and it certainly wasn't good for my fingernails.

So I bustled Jane's nurse into the room without the slightest idea of what she was going to do — and suddenly I thought of clothes. Of course! Jane and her sister Katherine would have to have something to wear to the coronation.

The nurse immediately whisked over to a trunk, opened it, and took out Jane's and Katherine's best dresses, which they hadn't worn for a year. Then, of course, Jane's dress would be too small for her, so that would create a problem. Then, of course, Jane would be dejected because her younger sister was so much prettier than she was, and looked as if she would be so much more at home at court than Jane would be . . . and so on and so on.

I ended up changing and shortening what I wrote — a lot of it just blathered on — but the exercise got the creative juices flowing and I was writing again.

Something else that works: if I'm well and truly stuck, I'll take what I've already written and rewrite it. It's going to be rewritten anyway, so it's not time wasted.

Again, just the act of writing and getting your mind involved with your story will likely carry you past the dead spot. I often find that by the time I arrive at the point where I'd stopped writing before, I'm ready to sail right on.

I'll let you in on a secret. I'd finished the whole manuscript for this book when my editor called me and said he wanted one more chapter — a chapter on what to do if you get stuck.

My immediate reaction was, "Oh, no! I don't want to write on what to do when you get stuck. I have enough trouble with that myself without trying to advise others about it."

"Try. See what you can do," the editor said.

So I followed my own advice and sat down at my typewriter. (This was in my pre-computer days.) Guess what? I was stuck. Thoroughly stuck. I got up, walked around the room a bit, looked out the window, and discussed the matter with my cat who, not being a writer himself, wasn't too interested.

Then I put my mind to work and tried to remember all the times when I'd been stuck before and how I'd become unstuck. Then I sat down again and started jotting down what I remembered on a piece of paper. Then I reread my manuscript. Then I turned back to the typewriter, started tentatively to type a few words and, much to my surprise, here we are!

Try This!

1. Get on with writing your story. If you get stuck, try some of the tips from this chapter — or see if you can come up with some of your own.

2. Still stuck? Try having a conversation with one of your characters. Ask him or her, "Is there anything you want to tell me?" You can even try sitting in a different chair, pretending to be the character, and seeing what pops into your mind.

3. If you're stuck because your "inner editor" has you stalled, tell it to be quiet. (Your inner editor can be recognized by such sayings as "I can't do this" or "This isn't good enough," and you need to keep a good rein on it! Tell it about the great character you've invented or the terrific dialogue you just wrote.)

Where are the brakes on this thing?

Almost as hard as starting — sometimes even harder — is knowing how and when to stop. With my Lady Jane book it was pretty obvious where the book was going to end. It was to go full circle, right back around to the beginning. Getting there, however, proved to be more difficult than I'd anticipated.

Towards the end, every day when my daughter came home from school she would ask, "Did you finish it today, Mom?" and I would have to answer, "Well, no, not quite yet. It's going to be a little longer than I thought."

Finally one day she said, "You know what the problem is, Mom? You just don't want to kill her off."

She was right.

Endings may be sad or happy, but they must make sense and they must satisfy your readers. You want people to love reading your story, to be sorry to finish it and to feel that the ending was just right.

You have to make sure that your main character has solved the problems (and don't let anyone else do it for him or her), that she or he has solved them in a logical way, and that there aren't any loose ends left lying around.

By the end of a good story, your main character will have changed in some way. He or she won't be the same person as in the beginning. The character will have grown up a bit, or learned something, or done something that's affected his or her life.

The main player in your drama will have been actively involved instead of just sitting by and watching things happen.

- ✘ Maybe the boy with the pup spends every cent he's been saving for a bike on an obedience course for his dog.
- ✘ By giving your friend a chance to explain — by trusting her — you discover the truth behind your argument.
- ✘ By the time your hero at last finds that rotten kid, he's learned a big lesson about responsibility. (He's also learned how to get angry, very wet cats out of toilets.)
- ✘ You've got a great idea for the ending of the pencil eraser story. You could have the poor hero — yourself or someone else — suddenly remember a TV show that she's seen, or a first-aid demonstration at school. She throws herself, stomach down, over a chair in her room as hard as she can and the eraser pops out. (This is beginning to sound more like a comedy!)

✗ Your hero has managed to save herself, and she's learned something in the bargain, if only not to chew on pencils — at least, not on pencils with erasers. When you're doing your research for this one, you'd better check with someone who would know to see if all this is actually possible. (If not, maybe this is the idea that ends up in the wastebasket.)

It's always fun to have a surprise ending after building up suspense all through a story. Let's get back to that noise in the kitchen.

You've decided to make your main character a boy named Tom, and you're going to write in the first person. It's almost dark and Tom is all alone in the house. He can't remember for sure if he even closed the back door, let alone locked it. There have been several burglaries in the neighbourhood.

There's another crash in the kitchen! Does he run? Does he try to get to the phone and call the police? Does he drag up enough courage to go and look? Let's say he does:

I took a deep breath.

"Don't be such a coward, Tom," I told myself, but I couldn't manage to convince my knees to stop shaking. I took another breath, then I opened the kitchen door.

The first thing I saw was a mess of broken dishes on the floor. The next thing I saw was a raccoon on the kitchen counter with his head in the cat-food bag. The cat was sitting on the counter right beside it, washing her face.

The back door *was* open, and Cleo had invited a friend in for supper.

We'd better not forget your teacher, stuck there with all those walls falling down around him. *Of course* you rescue him — at great risk to your own life and limb. And *of course*, as soon as he's well enough to come back to school he expects that story to be handed in.

The boy who had the dream about being trapped in the fire? What if, the next night, he wakes up to find the house is *really* on fire? And what if he gets out, then realizes his dog is in the kitchen and starts to go back in for her, then remembers his dream. He stops himself just in time. (And of course, the dog gets herself out and is perfectly safe.)

What about the doorbell? I can hear you asking. Well, it's been ringing and ringing, and you are so busy with something really important that you just can't stop and go to answer it. Nobody else seems to be going either, however; so finally, with a huge sigh of exasperation, you go.

It's the mailman. Bringing you a registered letter with a cheque in it from a magazine that has just bought your very first story!

Try This!

1. Write that ending to your story. Write it over and over until you get a satisfied feeling inside you that says: "Yes! That's the way it should be."

2. If you get a voice saying "So what?", first make sure it isn't just your inner editor being negative. Try to identify exactly what isn't quite working:

   Did your main character's conflict not get resolved? Does the ending seem to fizzle rather than conclude? Do you have major questions left unanswered? First deal with these concerns, then go back to Step 1 and work on your ending again.

The trouble with titles

Unfortunately, books and stories have to have titles. I find making them up hard — sometimes almost impossible. When I start on a new story I rarely know what the title is going to be. Because I'm a fairly neat and orderly person, however, I like to see a title on the first page, so I stick something up there and call it my "working title." In the course of writing the story it usually changes several times.

The trouble with titles is that they have to do so many things. First of all, they have to tell people what the book or story is all about, or at least give a hint. But, at the same time, they can't be boring.

They have to be catchy or interesting. They can't be corny, they can't be dumb, they can't be drippy. The author has to be comfortable with them. A title that has great meaning for the author, however, may mean nothing at all to someone else. It's no wonder that I'm not alone among authors in often putting off the naming of my books and stories until the very end. I found naming my children easier!

My first book was called *A Year for Growing*. The story is about a boy named Robbie who had to spend a year with his grandfather, and they didn't get on at all well. During that year they both changed and did a lot of growing. I didn't think of that title until I'd finished two drafts of the book.

Then, when the book was reprinted, the publisher decided it needed something snappier. It took me weeks. Finally, when I was doing a reading from the book to a school class, it suddenly hit me that Robbie felt that everything he did at first in this new and strange environment was wrong.

Out of the clear blue sky (or the well-lit classroom) the title *Wrong Again, Robbie* just jumped out at me, and that's what the book is now called. The publisher was right, because when I ask, most kids prefer the second title. I even had one boy come up to me once and tell me that he'd bought the book because his name was Robbie and he was always wrong, too.

When I wrote a ghost story, my working title was *The Summer the Dolphins Came*, and I still like it best, although I can see that it wasn't too informative. There had to be something in the title to let people know it was a ghost story, so it became *The Haunting at Cliff House*.

Perhaps the easiest time I ever had with a title, and the only time that the title I started with stuck with the book all through, was when I wrote *The Other Elizabeth*. It's about a girl named Elizabeth who goes back through time and takes the place of another girl named Elizabeth.

That one was easy. The one that came after wasn't so bad, either. In that book, another girl finds in a meadow a mysterious stone that has the power to transport her back in time. The title was simply *The Stone in the Meadow*, although it did take me a while to think of it.

The next book was a killer. I'm not quite sure how many titles I went through on it, each worse than the last. I remember only one of them, *Journey into Tomorrow*, and that's so bad I have no wish to look back in my records to find out what the others were.

It wasn't until I was well on into the book that I stumbled on the right title. Rachel, the heroine, is very unhappy. She's made the unicorn the symbol in her own mind of all that is perfect and beautiful in the world, but, just as unicorns don't really exist, so she feels perfection and beauty will never really exist for her, either.

At one point she says, "I wish there *were* unicorns." As soon as she said it I knew that had to be the title of the book.

My story about the three-legged dog didn't get its title until I typed the very last words. At the end, when Jeff sees his dog sitting there in the winners' circle, and people are standing up and cheering, he realizes that his dog *is* a champion after all, just *A Different Kind of Champion*.

There are some tricks you can do to make your titles interesting. Alliteration is one — words that start with the same sound, whether or not they start with the same letter. *Wrong*

Again, Robbie is an example of that; so is the title of this chapter.

Or you could make your title a question. I did that in a short story about a girl who was faced with a choice of which way she was going to go to school, on a morning when she was already late. The whole of the rest of her life depended on the choice that she would make. I called that story *Which Way?*

You could make your title so unusual that it's intriguing. I called one short story *Coffee, Snacks, Worms*. I like to think nobody would be able to resist reading that one, if only to find out what the title means. Make the title contradictory. *To Last, You Have to Be First*, for example. Why not try a line of dialogue? *"I Hate You, Sue Parker!"* might make a good title.

Titles can give the reader a clue to what the theme of your book is. I wrote a book about the very first crusade of all, the People's Crusade. In it, I imagined the out-of-control crusaders pouring across Europe like a pack of starving wolves. I used the wolf as a symbol and an image all through the book — both of evil, and as a much-misunderstood animal. The title, *There Will Be Wolves*, came easily and naturally into my mind.

I had more trouble with the sequel, which is about the First Crusade. I went through many titles, trying to find one that would have something to do with the terrible ordeal that Theo, the young French knight who is the hero, has to go through. He begins by being eager to fight the

Holy War, but at the end he is disillusioned with war and wishes desperately for nothing more than a lasting peace when he would never have to fight again. As I reread my manuscript I realized that the main symbol I had used in this story was Theo's sword. At first gleaming and new, by the end, bent and broken. That's when the title, *Shadows On a Sword*, came to me.

One day a few years ago, I was struggling to think of a title for a small book I was writing for young people on how to write.

The day started out with me calling up to my son for the third time, "Chris! You're going to be late for school. Get out of bed right now!"

During the day I worked on my book.

After school it was my son's job to walk the dog. (Yes, still the same dog.)

"Chris," I reminded him, "don't forget to walk the dog."

"Later, Mom," he answered.

"No, not later. Right now!" I growled.

By dinnertime I hadn't yet come up with a title for that book. I called Chris to dinner.

"Be there in a minute," was the answer.

"Dinner's ready right now!" I shouted back.

Then something struck me. How many times a day do kids hear those words, "right now"?

And here I am right now, trying to write a book telling kids how to write . . .

How about . . .?

For a title . . .?

WRITE NOW!

Try This!

1. If you haven't already decided on a title, now is the time. Write down all the possible titles you can think of. Live with them for a while, then decide which one really fits your story best.

2. Think about your audience. How old are they? Will they be mostly boys, or girls? What main words from the story are punchy or catchy? What will grab your audience's attention? What's "the hook"?

3. Try your title out on some friends. Is it grabby? Does it urge them to read the story? If they don't know what the story's about, does the title get them interested, or is it too vague? (You have to remember that readers know nothing about your story yet, so the title has to be something that catches their attention without depending too heavily on what's in the story.)

Revision — it's not a dirty word

~~The first~~ drafts ~~of my manuscripts~~ usually look like this. ~~Very messy.~~ So messy that probably no one except me could ever read them.

Even though I write directly onto a computer now, and do a lot of my revising as I go along, I still print out regularly, and do a lot of revisions on the printed paper. They're still just as messy as when I wrote with a pen or on a typewriter. And that's fine. Because first drafts are for your eyes only. The main objective is to get your story down on paper — beginning, middle and end. I don't think I've ever started a story or a book without a dreadful, panicky feeling that I'm not going to be able to finish it.

In fact, I usually stay fairly panicky right up until the end. Only then, when I've typed in the very last period, can I relax and heave a sigh of relief. My story is down on paper! It's rough, it's sketchy, it still needs a lot of work, but it's *down* there. The hard work is over. Now I can start to play.

It may sound strange to you to hear someone speak of revision as play, but in a lot of ways it really is.

You can look at your story carefully and see

where it needs improvement. Perhaps you should explain something a little better. Perhaps you've spent too long describing something else and have interrupted your story. Perhaps the dialogue in one part sounds stilted.

Now's the time to go over everything and polish that story until it's absolutely the best that you can make it. (If you have time, try leaving your story for a week or two, to get some distance from it, then reread it. It may be easier to spot the areas that need revising.)

Have you ever stopped to think about what the word revision means? It is, literally, re-vision — seeing something again. That's what you will be doing now: looking at your story carefully for the second time and seeing what needs to be done to it.

Without the worry of "how is it going to end?" and "how am I ever going to get this written?" it really is a time to enjoy.

There are limits, of course. I wrote my first book several years ago. I sent it out to a publisher; the publisher sent it back. I sent it out again, and again the big, brown, bulky envelope came back. I decided that maybe I'd better reread it. It was now almost a year since I'd written it.

I reread it, and to my horror found that it wasn't nearly as good as I'd thought. So I sat down and rewrote it. (We're talking about a full-length book here. That's a lot of work.) Sure now that it was good enough to be published, I sent it out. Back it came.

To cut short the pain of remembering, I'll tell you that over the next six years I sent that manuscript out six times — and six times it came back. I rewrote it entirely three times, and bits and pieces of it I don't know how many times. It was getting pretty discouraging, especially since I'd written four more novels in those six years, and they were coming back too!

Finally, I sent it out one more time. When the mailman brought that disgustingly familiar brown package back yet again, I couldn't even bear to look at it. It lay on the hall table all day while I went around feeling very sorry for myself. It wasn't until late afternoon that I opened it. Sure enough, there was my manuscript — but this time an editor had written me a letter.

"Your manuscript is *almost* good enough to be published," he said, "but it needs a bit more work."

MORE WORK?

He then proceeded, for three single-spaced, typewritten pages, to make suggestions.

My first reaction was that if I had to rewrite that manuscript again, I'd be sick. My second reaction was that if an editor had bothered to take the time to write me such a helpful letter, it would be pretty dumb of me not it give it one more go.

Then I started thinking seriously about his suggestions and in spite of myself found I was getting enthusiastic all over again. Suddenly I couldn't wait to get going on it.

Dinner was late that night.

"You write well about animals," he had said. "Why not put in more about them?"

Robbie's grandfather had a wonderful hunting dog. What if Robbie turned up with a cat?

"Put in something about Robbie's school," the editor had said.

I didn't know exactly what I was going to do about that, so I just walked Robbie up to the front door of the school and decided to see what would happen. What happened was that two boys suddenly appeared (one of them called King-Size because he was so short) and they immediately became Robbie's very good friends — and major characters in the story.

How could I ever have left them out in the first place? When I'd finished rewriting the manuscript this time, it was a much better book — and the publisher accepted it.

✳ ✳ ✳

One very helpful tool when you're revising is your computer. Quite often after I have finished a chapter or a couple of pages, I realize that some of the paragraphs or sentences should be changed around. Perhaps my last paragraph should come in somewhere near the beginning, or something else that I wrote would work better later on in the story. When I wrote on a typewriter I would cut out the pieces that I wanted to change and then staple them into the place where I wanted them. That method will do, but if you work on a computer, changing things around is much easier. You select the section you want to move and then use the Cut and Paste command to move it. Word processors are different, of course, but all of them have a tool for this.

Search and Replace is a wonderful tool. When I finished the final draft of *The Nine Days Queen*, and had spent weeks typing up the good copy of the book, I found out to my horror that somebody I had called Sir all the way through should have been Lord. I had to go through and change the title every time it occurred. Unfortunately Lord has one more letter than Sir, so I had to retype pages and pages. It took me two more weeks to do it. Now, with a computer, if you realize one word is wrong all the way through your story, you just Search and Replace. Again, computer software packages are different, but they all have programs to do this.

It's particularly useful if you have to change the name of one of your characters, or if you realize you have misspelled a name. This happened to me in *There Will Be Wolves*. I had called one of my characters Almaric, and then realized the name should be spelled Amalric. I just gave my computer the command to replace the misspelled name with the correct one, every time it occurred, and in less than a minute it was done.

You can find your way through your manuscript with the Search command, too. Just use it to locate a key word (try a fairly unusual word, one that's not used too often in your story) and you won't waste your time scrolling through, looking for it.

If you are writing away and a word suddenly sounds horribly familiar, and you begin to suspect that you have overused it, key it into the Search command and see how many times it comes up. If you find that you have used the same word several times, unless you've done it on purpose and for a good reason, that's boring and bad style. Look it up in your thesaurus and find some synonyms to lighten and brighten up your prose. (Be careful, though. You might find a perfectly beautiful word in your thesaurus and be very tempted to drop it into your story, but if you do, read the passage aloud and listen to make certain that it fits in with the rest of your writing.)

I love the Delete command. It gives me such a feeling of power. If I am having trouble writing a certain section, I'll write it two or three times, see which version I like the best, and then Delete the others into cyberspace.

As you are writing, you may come up with ideas or descriptions that you can't use in the story you are working on, but that you really like. Don't let them get lost, and don't depend on your mind to remember them. Make a new file in your computer and put them all in there. Or, keep a separate notebook for them.

One word of advice if you are writing on a computer: SAVE! Save often, as you go along, and *always* when you're finished writing for the day. I make a backup disk of everything I write, and at the end of each work period I save on the hard drive of my computer and on the disk.

✳ ✳ ✳

When you've finished your second draft (or third, or fourth) and you're confident that you've revised your story to the best of your ability, then you have to tidy it up. This is the time to get out the dictionary and the grammar book.

Check your spelling. Make sure every comma is in the right place and that your grammar would earn you an A in English class.

If you use a computer, use its spelling checker, but beware . . . the computer doesn't know everything! It doesn't know, for example, when you should use "they're" instead of "their." You may have used the wrong one, but all it knows is that it's spelled right, so it won't worry about it. Even after you've checked the spelling on the computer, you have to go over your story again and make sure everything is right. (If you're not good at spelling, find someone who is, and ask, beg, or bribe them to help you. And if you're great at titles or characters, you could swap *your* skills for *theirs*, too!)

✳ ✳ ✳

As you're revising, you might want to use proofreading marks. They'll help you note the places you want to make corrections, without lots of writing over or scratching out. Here are some of the most common symbols, and their meanings:

Sentence	Symbol	Meaning
The cat purring is	∽	transpose/ reverse order
The cat is purring.	⌐	delete
The catis purring.	#	add a space
The cat is purig.	∧	insert
THe cat is purring.	/ or *lc*	lower case
the cat is purring.	≡	capitalize
The cat is pur ring.	⌒	close up
The cat is purring⊙	⊙	add a period
The cat is purring.¶"Boy, that cat sure is loud," Jim says.	¶	new paragraph

Reading aloud is an excellent way to help you make sure your story is as good as it can possibly be. I always read my stories aloud to my kids when they were small. They gave me feedback on what worked and what didn't work. That was helpful. They're all grown up now and don't live at home any more, but I still grab them and read what I'm working on to them when they come home to visit. When no one at all is around, I read to my dog. She doesn't give me much feedback, mind you, but I pick up a lot of things that need fixing, just by listening to myself.

If you can find a good friend or two, whose opinions you respect, read your story aloud to them. Even better, form a writing group with a few of your friends who also like to write. I have three friends with whom I meet once a month. We read what we are working on to each other, and give each other constructive criticism.

It's frightening to read your work aloud, however, even to the best of friends. You feel like you're exposing your very insides to them — and what if they don't like it? Even worse, what if they laugh?

There's no doubt about it, reading your own work out loud is a scary thing to do at first, but if you can make yourself be brave enough, it's really worthwhile. As well as getting other people's opinions, you will hear your story yourself and be able to find things that you had overlooked. Do you run out of breath before the end of the sentence? Perhaps a comma or a period might help. Does that dialogue really sound right, or when you read it out loud is it difficult to say? Does it sound stiff? Are your friends really interested, or are they squirming around and looking a little bored? Perhaps your plot needs some more work.

If you have such a group, be sure you help the others in it as much as they help you. When you are going to make a comment about their work, first of all tell them what you liked about it. What was good. What worked, and why.

For example:
"I liked the way you described Jane getting lost in the woods. You showed how frightened she was and what she felt like."

If you have a criticism, make sure it's *constructive*. Just saying "I didn't like that" doesn't help anybody.

Instead say:
"I have a problem with the way you showed Jane talking to her mother after she finally got home. I thought maybe she'd be so glad to be home, she wouldn't be mad at her mother any more. Wouldn't she even cry a bit?"

That's the kind of criticism that will help you, and that's how you can help your friends who are brave enough to read their work to you (and who are undoubtedly just as scared!).

✳ ✳ ✳

It's time to make the final copy. You've really worked on that story. It deserves the very best presentation you can give it. Do it credit by making it *look* as good as it is.

Whether you use a typewriter, computer, pen or pencil, the final copy should be as near to perfect in appearance as possible — everything neatly set up; titles, page numbers and your name in their proper places; not a smudge or a crossed-out letter anywhere.

Try This!

1. Play around with your story. Maybe add something. Maybe take out something that is boring or stops your story dead in its tracks.

2. Read it out loud to a friend or to your writing group or buddy.

3. Revise, polish, and check your spelling and grammar.

4. Write, type or print out a final copy that is just as good as you can make it.

Now sit back and admire your work. You've done it. You're finished. Look at that manuscript in front of you and tell me you don't feel proud. It may not have been easy — nothing worthwhile ever is — but it wasn't all *that* hard, was it?

Helpful
hints

Story Starter Ideas, and Writing Tips, from Some of Your Favourite Authors

Write a letter to an imaginary friend to tell that friend what's happening in your life — or your cousin's life, or your dog's life, or your iguana's life (even if you don't have an iguana). If the truth needs rearranging, do it. If made-up parts make the story better, add them. Throw your ingredients into the pot and stir!

—*Jo Ellen Bogart*
Author of *Two Too Many*,
Gifts, and *Mama's Bed*

If you have trouble ending your stories, why not start them at the end? Make up a great last line and then work *backwards*, asking yourself questions like: How could this happen, what kinds of characters could this sort of thing happen to?

—*Paulette Bourgeois*
Author of the popular Franklin series
and *The Amazing Dirt Book*

Get your writing partner, then use a dictionary to make a list of ten words each, words which are new to you. Then exchange papers and, without looking up the definitions of the words, write a short story using every word on your partner's list. Share your stories, and only then look up the real definitions.

—*Christiane Duchesne*
Author of
Who's Afraid of the Dark?

How to write a funny story? Create a ridiculous character, then put that character in a ridiculous situation (for example, knocking over a vase on a class trip to the museum). Then include a slapstick element by involving a person in authority. Try it!

—*Martyn Godfrey*
Author of *Why Just Me?* and
Do You Want Fries With That?

Clip a collection of human interest stories from the newspaper. Then mix the clippings up, select two at random and write a story that ties them together. Where the two ideas intersect, the story begins.

—*Monica Hughes*
Author of *Hunter in the Dark*,
The Isis Trilogy, *Castle Tourmandyne*,
Log Jam, and *Invitation to the Game*

Create a team to play your favourite sport.
Who are the stars? the duds? the crazy
personalities? How far can they go? All the
way to the championships?

—*Gordon Korman*
Author of the Macdonald Hall books,
Why Did the Underwear Cross the Road?
and *The Twinkie Squad*

Do some research on something you know
nothing about, then include it in a piece of
writing. Interview someone at a police station
to find out more about police procedures; call
a factory and ask for a tour of the assembly
line; contact a worker in a fast food restaurant
and ask to see what they do on an average
day. The more you learn, the more interesting
your writing will be.

—*Paul Kropp*
Author of *Moonkid and Liberty*,
Wilted, and *You've Seen Enough*

Choose a minor character from a favourite
story and write a diary for that character. As
you write, you'll begin to see your character as
a whole, real person.

—*Jean Little*
Author of *Mama's Going to Buy You a
Mockingbird* and *Hey World, Here I Am!*

To train yourself as a writer, you have to have eyes like a painter's eyes: you need to look at things and be able to describe them. Every day, describe something new. Use the best few words you can find in your description.

—*Janet Lunn*
Author of *Double Spell*
and *The Root Cellar*

If you want to write a story, tell it to three different friends first, then write it down. This will help you work out all the bugs.

—*Robert Munsch*
Author of *The Paper Bag Princess*
and *Love You Forever*

Interview your grandmother or grandfather or some older person you know and do a little story research. What were their lives like when they were your age? What did they wear? What sports or games did they play? What important world events were happening then?

—*Barbara Smucker*
Author of *Days of Terror*
and *Underground to Canada*

Think of three unrelated things, then challenge yourself to somehow tie all three together in one story.

—*Cora Taylor*
Author of *Julie* and
Summer of the Mad Monk

Describe not only what you've seen, but also what can be heard, smelled, touched and tasted. Try to remember to include descriptions of all of the things your characters sense the next time you write a story.

— *Eric Wilson*
Author of the *Tom and Liz
Austen Mysteries*

For more story starter ideas check out *Meet Canadian Authors and Illustrators*, by Allison Gertridge, published by Scholastic Canada Ltd.

Creating a Terrific Title or Cover Page

Once you've finished making your story the very best it can be, you can experiment with creating a cover page or title page. If you have a graphics program on your computer, play around with different typefaces and sizes for the title and your name. If you don't have access to a computer, you can create your own type, or buy Letraset or lettering stencils from an art supply store to help you make your cover page look professional. Here are some tips to keep in mind:

↘ Plan your page, deciding how much space to give to the title, and how much to the author's name. Decide on the finished effect you want: serious, humorous, dramatic and so on.

ˎ Choose the typeface (the style of lettering) you want to use. To get ideas for this, take a look through your classroom or school library, check out books with themes similar to those in your story, and see what typefaces and designs those books used. Then try out or adapt the ones you like best, or use a typeface that's totally different, but that feels like it "matches" your story.

ˎ Borders are a good way to set off your title. Select a style that suits the theme of your story, and remember that simple borders are often more effective than fancy ones.

ˎ For ideas on lettering styles, check out *The Lettering Book*, *The Lettering Book of Alphabets* and *The Lettering Book Companion*, all published by Scholastic.

Getting Published

If you'd like to try to get your story published, The Canadian Children's Book Centre has a list called *Writing by Children — Where to Get It Published*. It's available to young writers for $1.00, from The Canadian Children's Book Centre, 35 Spadina Road, Toronto ON M5R 2S9. Be sure to send your request along with a loonie, plus a large self-addressed stamped envelope.

Karleen Bradford has lived all over the world, and now makes her home in Ontario. She is the award-winning author of many novels, including *Wrong Again, Robbie; The Haunting at Cliff House; The Nine Days Queen; The Other Elizabeth; I Wish There Were Unicorns; The Stone in the Meadow; Thirteenth Child; There Will Be Wolves;* and *Shadows On a Sword.* She has also written two books about animals who have performed amazing feats: *Animal Heroes* and *More Animal Heroes.*